Virna Woods

The Amazons

A Lyrical Drama

Virna Woods

The Amazons
A Lyrical Drama

ISBN/EAN: 9783744782753

Printed in Europe, USA, Canada, Australia, Japan

Cover: Foto ©Andreas Hilbeck / pixelio.de

More available books at **www.hansebooks.com**

THE AMAZONS

A Lyrical Drama

BY

VIRNA WOODS

MEADVILLE, PENNA

FLOOD & VINCENT

The Chautauqua-Century Press

ω ρ ccc xci

The Chautauqua-Century Press, Meadville, Pa., U. S. A.
Electrotyped, Printed and Bound by Flood & Vincent.

TO
MRS. MARY H. FIELD
OF
SAN JOSE CALIFORNIA
THIS BOOK
IS AFFECTIONATELY DEDICATED.

THE AMAZONS

DRAMATIS PERSONÆ

PENTHESILEA   THERSITES

ACHILLES   ÆNEAS

DIOMED   MESSENGER

CHORUS OF AMAZONS

ARGUMENT.

The Amazons, hearing of the death of Hector and the extremity of the Trojans, come, under the leadership of their queen, Penthesilea, to assist them. She challenges Achilles to single combat and is slain by him, but not before he has noted her marvellous beauty and great courage, and moved with sudden love, would have with-held the fatal blow. He laments over her death, and is taunted by Thersites, who speaks mockingly of the queen. Angered beyond endurance, Achilles turns upon him and slays him. Diomed, to avenge Thersites' death, steals the body of Penthesilea, which Achilles had returned to the Amazons, and casts it into the Scamander.

THE AMAZONS.

ACHILLES.

Slow are the gods to work the will of men.
A hundred times the moon has risen pale,
A little crescent boat that skimmed the waves
Of deeps unknown ; a hundred times has spread
Her silver sails on her adventurous course,
And as she drifted near her journey's end,
Drawn them again and trembled into rest.
And thrice a thousand times the splendid car
Of day has glittered on the mountain's brow,
And the swift steeds have swept its noiseless wheels
Through the cerulean spaces of the sky.
And thrice a thousand times the calm-browed night
Has risen majestic from the unfathomed depths
Of subterranean being and let fall
Quiet and cooling shadow on the earth.
The birds have nested, brooded, flown again,
Nine times ; the beasts have mated in their lairs,
And their young range the echoing woods no more.
Our children, lisping at our knees, have grown
To youths and maidens, strong and beautiful,
And yet we linger on the plains of Troy.
Nine years the Achaean hosts have sacrificed

With pious rites to all the Olympians,
And promised stately temples, household shrines,
And wayside altars, if they will but give
The city to our hands ; and still we wait,
While Priam reigns within his stately halls,
And fall our heroes to the joyful hymns
And notes of laughter within the Trojan gates.
Well that we turned their hearts for once to grief,
With Hector slain ; well that we hear the wails
Of women for their husbands who went forth
Haughty and strong, to widow waiting hearts
In Hellas ; we have smitten heavily,
And victory will follow it erelong.
How many of our noblest have they heaped,
Stained with the dust, upon the battle-plain?
Thou knowest, Diomed, how many left
The fertile fields and busy streets of home,
Whose feet will tread familiar ways no more,
Lost in the mazes of dark Pluto's realms.
Thou knowest how we are aliens from the land
We love, brought hither on a fruitless quest,
Empty the house of Menelaus still,
And Helen yet within the walls of Troy.
Sad is my heart for all my comrades lost,
Heavy and sad that we must battle more;
Since years agone the city should have lain,
Ashes and ruins, and her people fled
Swift from our spear-points and the following flame.

DIOMED.

Nay, be not sad, Achilles, have we not
Brought low the mightiest of the enemy,
Avenged our heroes slain with princely sons
Of Priam, and the greatest of the race?
Nor speak complaining of the all-seeing gods,
Who often mingled with us in the fight.
Thou surely dost remember our great deeds,
That time Sarpedon slew Tlepolemus,

And Pallas moved beside us on the field.
Our swords were winds and drove the foe as dust,
Confused and dense and settling on the plain
Beneath our strokes ; they were storm-winds and beat
Back from the shore into an unknown sea
The mighty breaking billows of the war,
That thundered heavily and gathered up
Their strength against us only to succumb
Into the ebb-tide's sobs and murmurous moans.
Ay, they were rains and tempests that fell down
On flower and fruit, and left the field despoiled ;
They were a blight that gathered all to soon
The purple vintage of the fallen ranks.
Dost thou forget the steeds celestial won
That day from great Æneas, when he fell
And would have perished had not Venus borne
Her son beloved from the battle-field ?
Oh ! we were eagles, and the timid broods
Of Ilium's nestlings drove with broken wings
Back to their shelter ; while the god of war,
Like a great vulture, hovered o'er the dead.

ACHILLES.

Enough ; my soul responsive leaps to thoughts
Of war and conquest ; I would test the arms
Of mightiest heroes ; sweeter is the fight
To noble hearts than home and ease and love.
In battle we are gods, for we subdue,
And hold the power of life and death ; we feel,
Lifting the spear above the prostrate foe,
As the Olympians when they look to earth,
And say, "This man shall die and that one live."
Oh ! we are drunken with the wine of power ;
Raised with the magic of the ruddy draught
From grovellers of the earth to dizzy heights
Where only foot immortal dares to tread.
Peace is for women ; for the warrior, arms,
Glory, and conquest ; in the clash of shield

And point of spear is music for his heart:
And does he think of home, it is to go
Full of renown and honor to the sire
That sits in old age helpless and alone,
A ruined column crumbling to its fall.
But who are these approach the plains of Troy?
Has Ocean sent an army of white nymphs,
Or have the satyrs startled from the woods
Fleet-footed bacchanals that follow Pan?
Or from the mountains have the oreads,
Binding their tresses, left their lonely heights
And sylvan gods, to dwell below with men?
Or rather have the fountains and the streams
Given their limniad races to the earth?
So fair and beautiful are these who come,
Surely the off-spring of some source divine.

DIOMED.

Like fields of clover rippled by the wind,
Or like the crested foam on breaking waves,
They come, as white, as multitudinous.
Or like the million stars that nightly shine,
While in their midst hangs luminous the moon,
Her silvery glory brighter than them all,
They seem, with one, the fairest, at their head.
Lo! she might be the lovely archer-queen,
So white her arms, so fleet her glancing feet,
So bright, like ripened wheat, her shining hair.

ACHILLES.

Hark! they come singing and a battle-cry
Mingles with all the music of their words.

CHORUS.

"Zeu Soter, kai Nike,"
We look, Oh! Lord, to thee,
The lord of heaven and light,
To slay the sons of night,

To battle for the free.

Give victory to the right,
Uphold us with thy might,
  Who come a shield to be,
  A sword the oppressed to free,
And put their foes to flight.

And give thou victory,
To her who follows thee,
  Thou archer queen of night
  Thou maiden silver-white,
Whom mortals dare not see.

And thou, the goddess bright,
With shield and helmet dight,
  Whose worshippers are we ;
  Lend us who pray to thee
The aegis-bearer's might.

ACHILLES.

Their silvery voices linger in the air
Like echoes of the nymphs that haunt the streams
And dreamy coverts of Hellenic groves.

DIOMED.

Lo ! still they sing, and from their snowy throats
Come sweeter strains than from enchanted woods,
Or shores reverberant with siren songs.

CHORUS.

The maiden without stain
Forgot no wayside fane,
  And left no altar bare,
  To god of earth or air,
Or stream or stormy main.

Oh ! spirits everywhere,
Invisible and fair,
  Avenge through us the slain,
  Unloose the forged chain

A conquered people wear.

Nine years on Troy has lain
A curse of weary pain,
　Of battle and despair ;
　For her the shield we bear
And draw the sword again.

For her we bind the hair,
For her the conflict dare,
　For her on battle-plain
　We heap the mighty slain ;
Our cause be heaven's care.

ACHILLES.

Why come ye singing to the battle-plain ?
What would ye with Achaen warriors ? ye
Who seem like herald goddesses of morn,
So fair and beautiful, so fleet of foot ?

CHORUS.

For Troy the shield we bear,
For Troy we bind the hair,
　And draw the girdle up ;
　For Troy we spill the cup
In sacrificial prayer.

ACHILLES.

These are no nymphs, no goddesses of mirth,
But women warriors armed for deadly strife.

DIOMED.

'Tis Penthesilea and the Amazons.

CHORUS.

We come as wind and wave,
Swept from Æolus' cave,
　And blown across the deep ;
　We come to guard and keep
The city of the brave.

We come as storms that sweep
The valleys from their sleep ;
  We come to smite and save,
  To give what freedom gave,
With blood the sod to steep.

Let strife and carnage rave ;
The harvest that we crave,
  Our swords as sickles reap ;
  The noble slain we heap,
The plain with dead we pave.

Quiet for those that leap,
Laughter for those that weep,
  For those that slay, the grave ;
  And freedom for the slave ;
The spring-tide for the neap.

PENTHESILEA.

Where is the son of Thetis, he who slew
The valiant Hector, and around the walls
Of Priam's city dragged the hapless corse
Thrice with his chariot? Thinks he that the gods
Suffer such insult to the pious slain?
Where is the man that stained the warrior's deed
With private vengeance? Stands he at the head
Of noble warriors whose heroic deeds
Are heralded in high Olympian halls?

ACHILLES.

I am Achilles ; who art thou, fair queen,
For queen thou must be, great as beautiful.

PENTHESILEA.

Oh ! know ye not the warlike Amazons?
We are the bearers of the crescent shield,
Worshippers of the huntress Artemis,
Skillful with bow and arrow, strong of limb,
Fearless alike of all the race of men.

Our mothers reared us from our infancy
To war and hunting ; and we know the deeds
Of ancestors that make our powerful race
Illustrous and dreaded among men.
'Twas we that founded mighty Ephesus,
And built the temple to the archer queen.
The Asiatic hordes we drove before
Our glancing spears and raised the battle-axe
In arms made strong by high Olympian blood.
Our land is northward by the mighty sea,
And there where flows the river Thermodon,
The towers and ramparts of our capital
Reflect the glittering glances of the sun.
And I am Penthesilea, maiden queen,
Daughter of Ares, who upholds my arm
In battle, and makes good my deadly stroke.
No quarter do we either give or take ;
Prepare for combat, son of Peleus ;
For thee I seek upon the battle-plain ;
Thee would I offer to avenge the dead.

ACHILLES.

Nay, thou art formed for other battle-plains,
Womanly victories and bloodless strife.
None dare oppose thee if thou battle thus,
And willingly I yield me to thy might.

PENTHESILEA.

Ay, women's hearts do hunger after love,
As flowers that lift their thirsty faces up
To feel the dew ; and yet, methinks, oft-times,
There is a hunger of the soul that strives
After great deeds ; why would ye bar the way,
Pinion the mighty spirit if it be,
Perchance, enfolded in a woman's form ?
Do we not long for food and drink as ye,
Welcome the sea-wind blown across the plain,
Rejoice in light of day, and feel the blood

Leap to behold the grandeur of the storm?
Are we not subject unto birth and death,
Weary with labor, spent with fruitless pain ;
Know we not pity and anger, grief and love,
Even as ye? why should we then alone,
Unsatisfied, dwell thus apart and seek
Love to appease all hunger? why not fill
Our life with many and illustrous deeds,
Making our spirits mates for those we love?
True marriage is community of soul,
Thought, feeling, passion ; perfect harmony ;
And strains responsive to the skillful touch
Of love, blend in celestial melody,
Two separate chords united in a sound.

ACHILLES.

Enough, fair queen, for you would steal away
Men's reason with the music of your speech.
Woman's best logic is the witchery
Of grace and beauty and melodious voice.
By these she casts a spell about men's hearts,
And makes them ready servants to her will.
But much I wonder you have come to Troy.
What heralds took you tidings of the deeds
Of battle-plains? Why left ye peaceful halls
To mingle with the strife on foreign shores?

PENTHESILEA.

The thunder of the war across the sea
Rolled heavily and shook the peristyle
Of Amazonian warriors, and they rose
From love's embrace and children's clinging hands,
And girdled up their garments and put on
Their sandals ; and with mighty sword and shield,
They sped with swift feet winged like the winds ;
And like the winds that sweep across the land,
Heavy with storms, are come to smite the strong,
Who heaped their insults on the noble slain.

Oh ! heard we not the sad Andromache,
With loosened raiment and dishevelled hair,
Surrounded by her sorrowing maidens, wail
To heaven, while her orphaned infant's cry
Blended its shrill note with her loud complaint?
Thus have I heard a storm upon the deep,
With fearful roarings sweep its awful track
Across the waves ; when breaks a sudden sound
Of high-voiced winds that, sobbing, die away.
We saw the desolation in the halls
Of Priam's stately palace, and the gloom,
Where erst the hearth-fire glowed and fountains
    leaped,
Mid bowers of fragrance ; and the hero lay,
Returned from battle, on the silken couch,
Broidered by skillful fingers of his bride ;
Where the king's fifty children came and went
Rejoicing in the prowess of their arms ;
Thrice happy and thrice blessed in the walls
Of home, the bloody battle all forgot
In the soft glances of fond women's eyes,
And innocent prattle of their infant sons ;
Where cakes were burned and ruddy goblets spilled
Upon the altars of the household gods,
And at the dawning, joyful paeans rose ;
Where oft the marriage-torches lit the walls,
And oft to Hera offerings were made
In gratitude another child was born
To the great race of Priam.   Silent now
The morning hymn ; and smouldering embers strew
The hearth ; the women's fingers weave no more,
But rend the masses of their streaming hair.
All, all is desolate ; for Hector slain,
Rise wildest dirges and insistent prayers
To the high gods for vengeance.   All is changed,
As when above a blooming garden pass
Sear desert winds ; or over pleasant groves,
Dropping Jove's bolts of thunder, trails the storm.

ACHILLES.

Tell me not thus the sorrow in the halls
Of Priam ; tell me rather if you saw
Paris and Helen wandering side by side
With amorous words, or watched them sit apart,
Drinking the glances of each other's eyes.
The house of Menelaus, desolate
But for the slaves that wait their lord's return,
Speaks louder to my heart than all the tears
And fruitless wails of Priam's fifty sons.
And tell me if you saw Patroclus fall
Like fruit unripened that the hurrying wind
Dashes to earth ; his strength and beauty lost
To sate the anger of the men of Troy.
As thou art beautiful, be also just
And to the oppressor offer not thy aid.
As thou art maiden, lift not up the sword
For one who stole the virtue of a wife ;
As thou art woman, suffer not thy hand
To pierce a warrior-breast with deadly steel.
I would not stain thy white limbs with the dust,
Nor dim the lustrous beauty of thine eyes ;
I would not redden with thy ruby blood
The gleaming fairness of thy breast and brow.

PENTHESILEA.

The Amazons are brave and strong of arm
And ask not mercy of the haughty Greek.
But fear thou, for the gods are on our side.
Did they not look with pity and anger down
From out the golden parapets of heaven,
While swept thy chariot round the walls of Troy,
Dragging brave Hector's body in the dust?
Oh ! thinkst thou not Andromache was sad
With longing for the beauty of his eyes,
And blood-stained fairness of his breast and brow ?
Oh ! thinkst thou not she wept to see the dust

Stain all his whiteness?   Even so some maid
Of Greece shall weep at hearing of thy fate.

ACHILLES.

Lift not thy sword, for I would spare thee. queen.

PENTHESILEA.

Lift thou thy sword, or perish at my hand.

ACHILLES.

Pause but a moment ; thou art wondrous fair.

PENTHESILEA.

My face no fairer than my arm is strong.

ACHILLES.

Thy arm was made for love and not for war.

PENTHESILEA.

Yet can it strike a sure and deadly blow.

ACHILLES.

Forbear ! forbear ! the Fates are on my side.

PENTHESILEA.

The gods for Penthesilea and for Troy !

CHORUS.

He reels from the stroke,
    He staggers and reels,
As the strong mountain oak
    That shivers and feels
The blast of the storm ;
    But again proudly stands
With straight, god-like form,
    And uplifted strong hands.

ACHILLES.

Yield, I will spare thee, noble Amazon.

PENTHESILEA.

Nay, I will strike thee with a surer blow.

ACHILLES.

Alas! then must my heaven-made sword meet thine.

CHORUS.

The maiden advances,
  They grapple and fight ;
The blades of their lances
  Are flashes of light.
She has stricken his shield
  From the might of his grasp ;
But she sinks on the field
  With a moan and a gasp.

She is fallen, our queen,
  She is fallen and slain ;
Where her prowess was seen
  On the red Trojan plain,
Like a white flower she lies,
  As pure and as fair ;
But with night on her eyes,
  And with dust in her hair.

PENTHESILEA.

Achilles, this day have the high gods defended
The might of thy arm and the combat is ended.
Yet spare me the shame of dead Hector, I pray,
Lest the gods in their anger should smite thee and
  slay.

CHORUS.

Let us bear her away
  From the field of the fight,
While the heavens are gray
  With the coming of night.

You will build you a fire

And the sacrifice spread,
But the Trojans a pyre
For the rites of the dead.

PENTHESILEA.

I bend to the will of the gods ; who can raise
A snare for their feet or a bar to their ways ?
They veil them in splendor and hide them in light,
But for us is the darkness and gloom of the night.

CHORUS.

By the hand of Fate our doom is written
  In blood-red letters on Time's dark scroll ;
We fall by the breath of the high gods smitten,
  And darkness gathers about the soul.
We seek the gods and we follow after,
But cry in vain ; for Olympic laughter
Echoes in heaven from hall to rafter.

The way is dark and the path is lonely
  Our feet must travel in silence and night ;
If the gods in their bright abodes would only
  Give us a gleam of their golden light,
Safely the soul would pass the dim places
Into the deep unfathomed spaces
Where dead men walk with shadowy faces.

ACHILLES.

Sweet Amazon, fain would I give back thy breath ;
But fear not dishonor will follow thy death.
Thy comrades shall close the white lids of thine eyes,
And above thee the smoke of the sacrifice rise.
And over thy ashes a mound they shall raise,
Nor thy soul wander homeless on desolate ways.

CHORUS.

He lifts her, he holds her
  Fast sinking to rest,
His strong arm enfolds her,

She lies on his breast.
His eyes like a lover's
Are hot and afraid ;
With her tresses he covers }
The wound he has made.

ACHILLES.

Fairest of queens, couldst thou but live again,
Sooner my sword would sever my right hand
Than it should drink the red draught of thy blood,
Dim the twin constellation of thine eyes,
And part thy sweet lips with thy passing soul.
Wert thou not dying, I would speak fond words,
Tell thee how lovely the Hellenic fields,
And tempt thee back with me from bloody wars.
But what can Love avail when death is near?
I call in vain, I can not see her face,
But only the deep darkness of thy night.

CHORUS.

Oh ! Love once fled from the Fate that follows,
O'er rugged path-ways, through mist-hung hollows ;
Swifter her feet than the wings of swallows,
　　But swifter far were the feet of Fate.

Oh ! seek her not in Olympic places,
Nor among the perfect, immortal faces.
You will find her dead with the woodland races,
　　And her olden coverts desolate.

ACHILLES.

Alas ! 'tis true ; for me no more will shine
Through the dark nights the glory of Love's eyes.

CHORUS.

Hark ! men mourn her with paeans tragic ;
Only the touch of youth has magic
　　To waken once more the tremulous breath.

ACHILLES.

My hand will quicken not to life again ;
For me she sleeps with Penthesilea dead.

CHORUS.

Over the white of the rose's petals,
Dimly a shadow phantasmal settles ;
    The queen and thy love are one in death.

PENTHESILEA.

To die is sweet when sheltered in thy arms ;
And yet, indeed, it had been sweet to live,
And follow thee to thy Hellenic home.
But the gods, jealous that they gave us breath,
And made us love and joy even as themselves,
Stir in our draught of life a bitter herb,
And dash the unemptied goblet from our lips.

CHORUS.

We have known thee, O, Life ! thou art sweet
To the lips as the heart of a flower ;
But the breath of thy perfume is fleet,
And thy joy is the bloom of an hour.
We have known thee, O, Life ! thou art fair,
But thy beauty the Sirens had ;
And stained are the robes thou dost wear ;
We have known thee, O, Life ! thou art sad.
We have known thee, O, Life ! thou art strong ;
Thou art strong, and thy burdens are great ;
We have feared thee and worshipped thee long,
For thy form is the shadow of Fate.
Thou hast given us faith as a gem ;
It was lost in the flush of the morn ;
And virtue, a garment whose hem
Was unspotted, the storm-winds have torn.
Thou hast given us love as a flower ;
It has withered and died on the breast ;
Thou hast given us riches and power ;

They have vanished as foam from the crest.
Thou hast given us hope as a staff;
It is trampled and broken by fears;
And the red wine of pleasure to quaff;
It is darkling, and bitter with tears.
Thou hast given us fame as a crown,
But hast tarnished its glory with rust;
Thou hast sprinkled the robes of renown
With the soil of thy ashes and dust.
We have known thee, O, Life! thou art fleet,
And the span of thy race is a breath;
We have followed the path of thy feet,
And the goal that thou seekest is death.

PENTHESILEA.

Farewell, sweet world; across the window, whence
I looked upon the beauty of the hills
And saw the sun rise and the twilight fall,
Is drawn the curtain, and I see no more.
Achilles, in your far Hellenic home,
When men shall praise the prowess of your arm,
Tell how you fought upon the Trojan field
And none could stand against your godlike power;
When your fair wife (some lovely Grecian maid
Now waiting breathless for the long war's end)
Shall lift your infant from her fragrant breast
And lay it, softly cooing, in your arms;
When life is full and brimming o'er with joy,
Think of me once with kindness and forget.

ACHILLES.

Ye gods, but hear my vows; I promise lambs
And spotless bullocks and the salted cakes,
With full libations on your altars poured,
Six days and nights, if ye will hear my prayer.
Snatch from the realms of Pluto this one shade,
Call back the soul that walks the shadowy road
To the dim river and the ghostly boat
Of Charon; hear me once before I die,

Let my feet never touch the blooming fields
Of Hellas more, if only she may live.
Zeus, thou wert not unheedful to the prayer
Of nereid Thetis, rising from the sea,
To clasp thy knees, a suppliant for her son.
Hear now that son, and many fanes shall rise,
And sacred altars, and a temple built
In Hellas, and thy image in the midst.
Alas! the gods will harken not my woe.
Would my good sword had found my throbbing
    heart,
Ere its steel cleft the snows of thy soft bosom,
And quenched the precious fire that burned within.
Sweet queen, the music of thy voice is hushed
As winds are silent on a broken lyre;
Thy body, like a temple grand and fair,
Despoiled of all the images within,
Empty and desolate; thy shining eyes
Deep hidden in a dark and starless night.

CHORUS.

To the wild forester
Sounds the wind chorister
   Breaking o'er mountains
     And blowing o'er seas;
Heaven sends rains to him
And the rich plains to him
   Offer their fountains
     And fruits of their trees.

Cares not for money he,
Hybla's wild honey-bee
   Gives him her treasure,
     The squirrel his store;
For fame unknown to him,
Pure joys atone to him;
   Full is his measure,
     He seeks not for more.

Though day is luminous,
Heaven sheds gloom on us,
  And the woods birdless
    But sigh to the wind ;
For our fair maiden queen
Now is dust-laden seen,
  Pallid and wordless,
    Unhearing and blind.

But her virginity
Sheds a divinity
  Over the features
    So lovely in death.
Would we could follow her
Where the shades swallow her ;
  We are but creatures
    Made heavy with breath.

Glory is powerless,
Beauty is flowerless
  In the dark places
    Where Pluto abides ;
Love's spontaneity
Shorn of its deity ;
  Darkened the faces
    Of lovers and brides.

In war victorious,
In battle glorious,
  With lance and with quiver,
    Walked proudly the maid.
Mid phantoms numberless,
Wandering slumberless,
  Homeless forever,
    Gropes lonely her shade.

ÆNEAS.

Oh ! what is this, most pitiful to see?
Just now I hastened through the Scaean gate,
Across the plain to where the combat raged,

Hopeful the Amazons, whose moving host
Seemed numberless, would strike a heavy blow
Upon the enemy ; but at their feet
Low lies the far-famed queen ; unhappy fate,
To sink amid her arms and clanging shield,
No more to lift the lance or throw the spear,
So young and lovely, on the battle-plain.

ACHILLES.

More beautiful and fair upon the field
Than in the heavens new-risen, the evening star ;
Sweeter than breath of flowers in summer winds,
Fresher than breezes from the occan blown
On thirsty fields, the maiden-warrior lies.
Lovelier than dawn upon the mountain-tops, ⌣
Fleeter than nymphs that flee and follow Pan,
Was Penthesilea ; silent now and cold,
Paler than limniad faces in the springs.

CHORUS.

Like a lily fallen
  Lies she there ;
Like the lily's pollen
  Is her hair.

Rise her face and bosom
  From her mail,
Like the perfect blossom
  Pure and pale.

ÆNEAS.

Like a lotus blooming
  In the reeds,
When, the shadows glooming,
  Day recedes.

Like a white uplifted
  Asphodel ;
Like its petals drifted
  As they fell.

THE AMAZONS.

CHORUS.

Why did we come hither
  To the fight,
Where the flower must wither
  In our sight?

ACHILLES.

Thou art a fallen cedar,
Thou art a wind-blown cypress,
Beautiful Amazon leader;
Yet a frail lily that I press
Rudely in impious fingers,
Over which, bruised and broken,
Exquisite fragrance still lingers,
Of its lost freshness the token.
Thou art the fairest and sweetest
Born of all women, completest;
To the Olympians nearest,
And to Achilles the dearest.
Thine were the lightest and fleetest
Of the swift feet in the chases ;
Thine were the fleetest and lightest;
Thine was the bosom the whitest;
Thou, of all maidens the rarest,
Lost to thy lover's embraces,
Thou art the sweetest and fairest.

CHORUS.

Vain is it we languish
  Desolate ;
Vain Achilles' anguish
  At thy fate.

Blossom perfect-moulded,
  Touched with night,
All thy heart is folded
  Out of sight.

ÆNEAS.

Vain the dirge and ditty
  That we sing ;
Vain the love and pity
  Of the king.

To the darkness bidden,
  Thou must sleep,
Like a jewel hidden
  In the deep.

CHORUS.

And for thee the chill is
  And the gloom ;
But for thine Achilles,
  Life and bloom.

ACHILLES.

Life without love is a lute
Wanting a touch on the strings ;
Perfect, but songless and mute.
It is a bird without wings,
Longing for deeps of the sky.
It is a soul without birth ;
It is a spirit of earth,
Yearning for infinite things.

Life without love is a night
Starless, unknown of the moon ;
Day, without dawning of light,
Shadows and darkness at noon.
It is a fountain gone dry ;
It is a weight on the feet ;
Embers of fire without heat ;
Words of a song without tune.

Life full of love is a stream
Lost in the ocean ; a leaf
Fading in crimson ; a dream.

Love, like a phantom of grief,
Spectral and dim, glimmers by,
Fails at the threshold of death,
Passes from man like a breath,
Leaves him alone on the reef.

CHORUS.

Sleep, thou peerless maiden,
  Nor awake,
Where the sorrow-laden
  Heart may break.

What to thee the battle
  And the field?
What the lance's rattle
  On the shield?

What the life-blood staining
  Dust with red?
Women's loud complaining
  For the dead?

Silence is around thee,
  And above;
Snapped the chains that bound thee,
  Fame and love.

Is the world without thee?
  It has been.
Darkness is about thee,
  And within.

All that now encumber
  Earthly sight
Soon will know the slumber
  Of thy night.

Soon their ears will hearken
  Ghostly hymn;
Soon their eyes will darken
  And grow dim.

Soon the urn will cover
   Up the cold
Ashes of thy lover
   And enfold

(But a transient story
   Of decay),
All his strength and glory
Passed away.

Full of striving, trouble,
   Mystery,
Man is but a bubble
   In the sea.

But a tree uprooted
   By the wind,
With his hopes unfruited
   Left behind.

But the storm-clouds' masses,
   And their flight ;
But a day that passes
   Into night.

ACHILLES.

Gone is the light from the sky,
   Gone is the music of earth ;
Silent the wind passes by ;
   Empty the houses of mirth.
For in my heart all have fled
   Out of its chambers and halls ;
   Only the ghostly foot-falls
Of hopes and of memories dead.

Love has departed with thee,
   Beautiful Amazon queen ;
Leaving the shadow with me,
   Only of that which has been.
And for the beauty of faith,
   And for the fragrance of joy,

(Oh! for these battles of Troy)
Only a ghost and a wraith.

Never with thee to abide,
   Empty and useless is life ;
Haply with thee for my bride,
   I would remember the strife
Only as dreams that are dreamed,
   Only as tales that are told ;
   Now all the joy that I hold
Is but a vision that seemed.

CHORUS.

Dies the deepest thunder,
   Fades the gleam ;
All is but a wonder
   And a dream.

ACHILLES.

As from the ocean come all founts and streams,
And seek again the waters whence they sprang,
So from the vastness of eternity,
Come rivulets of time, that bear frail barques
Of human life, and seek their ocean-home,
Losing their ripples in its larger waves ;
The mighty river that has borne the world,
Since first it wakened at the word of gods,
Flows on, a broadening current, to the sea.
We hear the music of its mighty waves,
The thunder of its dashing, and the play
Of its spent billows ; but we can not see
The ending of the stream ; nor far away,
In mist-hung summits, where its course began.
We watch the rising of the sun, and mark
Its upward path, and follow its descent
Below the earth ; but when we see the world
Slow moving in the orbit we call Time,
A broken arc is all that we behold.

A fragment only of the mighty whole
That orbs itself from ancient primal dawn,
To the yet distant mystery of night.
How small a thing is one poor human life,
In the majestic unity that makes
The human race ; and yet, when it is lost,
And like a sea-shell stranded on the shore,
Lies at our feet, we feel more bitter pain
Than for the mighty multitudes of dead,
The driftwood of unnumbered ages gone.
The heart loves what is near and beautiful,
More than the glory that is grand and far ;
The faces near and loved shut from our sight
The ranks of heroes and forgotten great ;
As a fair, fragrant flower held to the face,
Obscures a star ; or as a bird may hide,
With daring flight, the splendor of the sun.
But what were life without this nearer love,
That holds the mingled cup of joy and pain
To eager, thirsting lips? It were a thing
Of contemplation or of idle dreams ;
A homeless phantom of a winter night.
'Tis love transforms it to a radiant soul,
Breathes in it with the warm breath of the gods,
And clothes it in the garments of the dawn.
'Tis love that blossoms in the wastes of life,
Till all the chambers of the heart are full
Of fragrance and of beauty ; it is love,
That breaks the prison-barriers of the soul
And lifts it to the heights of being ; blest
Is he who plays on all the various strings
Of love and draws divinest harmony
Into the lofty paean of his life ;
The love of home, of kindred, and of friends ;
Allegiance to his country, and the pure
High worship of the gods ; and last of all,
That love that moved Endymion to rove
The woods beneath the glamour of the moon

Searching the heavens for one perfect face ;
That love that stirs the birds at nesting-time,
That penetrates the jungles in the deeps
Of haunted forests where the lioness
Dwells with her savage mate; that breathes through all,
Even the elements that blend and make
The visible universe, the earth, and air,
And sea ; the light, the darkness, and the storm ;
That love that makes all habitats its home,
But springs most beautiful in heart of man,
And links him to the grandeur of the gods.
Not as the stars that blossom one by one
In pathless fields, but as the sun that breaks
Full-orbed from morning clouds, it fell on me,
Full of all warmth and beauty ; then unrest
Woke in my heart, and tumult, and desire,
Too soon eclipsed in everlasting night.
All other loves were stars to this one sun,
And at its dawning faded from my heart.
All other feelings were but streams that flowed
Into this one emotion's boundless sea.
And now my heart, tossed ever on its waves,
Is but the plaything of the wind and storm.
Oh ! Love, that thou shouldst be so beautiful,
And yet so cruel, unfathomable, and sad.

CHORUS.

Oh ! Love, with wings of the dawn's bright hue,
   And sweeping robes of a spotless white,
Why is the air that thy breath passed through,
   Suffused with darkness and heavy with night ?

Oh ! Love, why art thou so wondrous fair,
   With the godlike form and the angel face,
With the light of heaven upon thy hair,
   And beauty that shines from thy dwelling-place ?

Thy voice is sweet as a siren's song,
   Thy words are promise of hope and joy ;

But the heart that hearkens thy music long,
  The winds and waves of thy wrath destroy.

ACHILLES.

Had I not met her on this fatal field,
Nor ever, under more auspicious skies,
Beheld her matchless loveliness, nor known
The greater beauty of her heart and mind,
Then had my heart, unwakened by the touch
Of love and longing, slumbered till the gods,
Grown weary of my deeds, had called my soul
To join the shadows ; blessed that I know
The face of Love, though only for such space
As lives the purple sunset in the sky,
It shone upon me ; better thus, than live
A thousand years of other lesser loves.
Now, Love, alas! so beautiful and brief,
With thy first touch upon me, I say farewell.

CHORUS.

Oh ! Love, thou art wind and the foam of seas,
  Thou art stars that fade and blossoms that die ;
Thou art storms and the wrath of Symplegades ;
  Thou art feet that run, thou art wings that fly.

Thy breath is a perfume, thy glance a light ;
  Thy touch is a spell star-fallen and brief
As the span of a fragrant summer night ;
  And the shadow that follows thy steps is grief.

Oh ! Love, thou art fair, thou art false and fleet,
  A shadow, a phantom, a nameless dream ;
A fruit that is bitter from flower that is sweet ;
  A fountain that dries, and a hidden stream.

ACHILLES.

What's left the heart when love and hope are flown ?
To live when all that makes life dear is dead ;
To walk with men, but be with them no more
In thought and feeling than the shadowy forms

That wander like the phantoms of a dream
In the dim twilight of the underworld.
To view familiar scenes with alien eyes,
To watch unmoved the splendors of the dawn,
Nor see in it a symbol of great deeds
That shed their glory over wondering worlds ;
To note, without a thrill, the moonbeams lie
Among the flickering shadows of the brakes,
Or touch with silver softness craggy heights
That round the valley stand like sentinels,
To tell the gods how fares the world below ;
To hear without a heart-throb all the winds
Making aeolian music to the night,
While hang the billows underneath the stars,
Pallid with gazing on the white-faced moon.
To breathe without delight the perfume borne
From fragrant haunts of faun and woodland nymph,
To bind my brow with garlands while the cup
Of Bacchus brings no pleasure; to lie down
On rose-strewn couches knowing but the thorns ;
To feel unstirred the sweeping of the wings
Whose flight is life ; and hear the lapsing stream
That sinks its waters in the ocean-flood ;
To wait for death as one who waits for sleep,
Through weary hours of sufferance and toil ;
To drop at last into the great abyss,
Without regret or longing for the world.
This, this is life, the best gift of the gods.
What's left the heart when love and hope are flown?

CHORUS.

To share the burdens of a hapless world,
To pour the healing oil of sympathy
On grievous wounds and aching scars of life ;
To warm the soul that wanders in the cold,
To light the feet that stumble in the dark ;
To offer holy prayers to all the gods,
And rise, renewed, from purifying fires

Of sacrifices given in worthy deeds.

ACHILLES.

What's left the hands when love and hope are flown?
Never to raise the loved one to my breast,
Never to bless her or to fondle babes
That climb my knee and lisp their father's name.
What's left the hands when love and hope are flown?

CHORUS.

To lift the spear in the defense of right,
To succor helplessness and smite the strong,
To pour libations to the living gods,
To point the way to valor and to truth.

ACHILLES.

What's left the feet when love and hope are flown?
Never to wander in the echoing aisles
Of wind-stirred forest or in mountain-glades,
While at the low words of the tender tale,
Her lips part and her bosom softly swells,
While her eyes tremble 'neath the dropping lids?
Never to walk Life's pathways by her side,
Never to linger for her halting feet,
Or lean perchance her weakness on my strength?
What's left the feet when love and hope are flown?

CHORUS.

To walk the heights before the eyes of men,
And upward striving, reach the knees of gods.

ACHILLES.

Sweet Love, your memory will live with me,
As echoes haunt the air where music dwelt;
Or as the twilight lingers after day.
Your glory will not from my life depart,
Till life itself drop silently to sleep.
The image of this maid within my heart

Will cast a halo on all deeds and thoughts,
And make them better for its presence there.

THERSITES.

Hear the brave warrior, Peleus' mighty son,
Lament as Trojan women o'er their dead.
His strong hands tremble and his cheeks are wet
With childish tears; I wonder not the gods,
Unheedful of his sorrow, laugh in heaven.
And who is she, this Amazon, this queen
Of women, weakling of a weakling race?
Foolish, she thought to lift her puny arm
Against the might of Hellas, and she died.

ACHILLES.

Dare not, rash men, to speak a mocking word
Of Penthesilea, bravest in the fight,
Nor of my sorrow, and the gods' disdain.

THERSITES.

Why should I honor this slain Amazon?
It is not meet that women should usurp
The paths of men and follow their high ways
With faltering feet; within the peristyle,
Weaving among their maidens, they should pass
The days that linger till their lords' return.
And for your sorrow, what is that to me?
How long did you, unmindful of us all,
Keep to your tent, apart from bloody fields,
Nursing your bitter anger with the king?
While in the fight the fair Achaean youths
And honored warriors fell amid the dust,
Like flowers unwithered that the strong wind breaks
Tearing their fragrant petals from the stem?
Only, indeed, your loved Patroclus slain
Could tempt you forth; 'twas not for Greece you
    fought,
But to avenge the slaughter of your friend.

And now, a pallid face and yellow hair
Make you forget the glory of the war,
And grieve before the brave victorious ranks,
As for a broken bauble cries a boy.
Cast down the body of the Amazon,
And let the vultures and the ravens feed
On the white beauty that ensnares your eyes;
Let her soul be the bride of sorrow, as
Her spotless body is the bride of death.

ACHILLES.

Since the gods silence not your impious tongue,
Withdrawn to banquet in their high abodes,
Unmindful of the heavy hearts of men,
And even Artemis sends not an arrow
To avenge the insults of this slaughtered maid;
Thus do I offer you a sacrifice
To Pluto and the fair Persephone;
Send your dark soul among the darker shades;
And may the vultures tear your jeering tongue,
And your ghost wander mourning by the shore
Of the dim river for a hundred years.

THERSITES.

Ye gods! I die beneath his ruthless hand;
But unavenged my spirit shall not go
To the dark shades and twilit house of death.
Ere long, when he has passed the shadowy stream,
And enters in the hollow noiseless realms
Of the grim Pluto, I shall meet him there,
Even at the threshold, and delight mine eyes
With looking on the proud Achilles, slain
By the weak hand of Priam's feeblest son.
Not vainly did thy mother Thetis choose
That thy career be brief and glorious.
The time draws near; Fate lifts her unerring hand;
Thy feet will tread Hellenic fields no more.

ACHILLES.

Silence thy vaunts; thou canst not prophesy.
Stain not the threshold of the great unseen,
Nor taint its breathless air with bitter words.
Swift thy dark spirit takes its pathless flight.
Thy lips are mute, thy tongue will jeer no more.

CHORUS.

Achilles, ever victor, stands
Above the slain with crimson hands
    And blood-bright sword;
And even Fate seems to with-hold
The strokes of slaughter manifold,
    From him, the battle's lord.

That soul the gods have loved and made
Of all life's dangers unafraid,
    And lifted high
A glorious pathway for his feet,
Will his high destiny complete;
    He lives, and shall not die.

So once, when Rhea hid, of yore,
The infant Zeus, wild pigeons bore
    From Ocean's spring,
Ambrosia; and an eagle drew
Nectar from rocks and, swift-winged, flew
    To heaven's fated king.

Nor shall the Achaean hero die
Before Hellenic battle-cry
    Rings in the walls
Of fated Ilium; and in fires
Of torches and of funeral pyres,
    The glorious city falls.

For us, we turn aside and go,
Idle as winds that cease to blow,
    Back to our home.
We proudly came like waves at tide,

Backward like waves at ebb, we glide;
Our queen, the broken foam.

ACHILLES.

Take ye your queen and build a lofty pyre,
Wrap her white limbs in softest rainment; shed
Perfumes about her; light the sacred fire,
And make ye offerings for the lovely dead.
Back to my tent I go with heavy thought
Of all my hand this fateful day has wrought.

CHORUS.

Back from the field of battle
Goes the illustrous victor;
Zeus and the gods upheld him.
Lift on your shields the dead maiden,
Spared by the conqueror's mercy.
Lift her and bear from the battle;
Build ye a pyre and the softest
Of raiment wrap round the fair body,
Sweetened with incense and perfume.
Let the priests all the rites render,
And let the women bewail her.

DIOMED.

Thersites, who will wail and weep for thee,
While Trojan women fill with lamentations
The halls of Troy? will proud Achilles raise
A pyre and place thine ashes in the urn,
And offer sacrifices to the gods?
Who will avenge thee for thy untimely death?
Who will avenge thee if it be not I?
Forgive me that I slew not him that slew,
But let the raging lion escape the snare.
Yet thou shalt be avenged; to Zeus I make
The awful vow, and to the darker gods
That rule the realms of shadows and of night.
What is't to me that this slain Amazon

Should touch the warrior heart? My friend lies low,
Not slaughtered by the enemy to win
Deathless renown and glory; but struck down
By one whose arm should have befriended him.
I go, but unforgotten thou shalt be.

SEMI-CHORUS.

Low she lies upon the sod,
Who the field of battle trod;
Blue eyes hidden like the sky
Over which the white clouds lie;
Bright hair fallen in the stain
Of the dust like scattered grain;
Bosom motionless and white
As the moon on summer night.
Quiet are the feet that ran
Fleet and well their little span;
Quiet are the hands that smote;
In the fair and fragile throat,
Silent is the wonted note;
And the cheek that blushed to know
Love and praise, is pale as snow.
Lips from which the color goes,
Lovely as the heart of rose,
All their honeyed sweetness hold,
Though they wither and are cold.
Beautiful, serene, and fair,
All we knew and loved is there,
But the spirit wont to dwell
Lovely and invisible.
Love is lost and life is past;
Only death and silence last;
Like a battle that is fought,
Like the memory of a thought,
Fallen petals of a rose,
Fading lines of melted snows,
Tide-marks on the gleaming sands,
Drifted clouds and broken bands,

Level seas where billows tossed,
Life is past and love is lost.

CHORUS.

Oh ! the sea was gray when the early mist
  Wrapped it heavily in a shroud ;
And the waves were red by the red dawn kissed,
  And myriad colors 'neath sun and cloud.
The waters amber at blaze of noon,
  Turned crimson under the sunset bars ;
And pale and ghostly beneath the moon,
  And black, when the vapors had hid the stars.
The blue and green of a cloudless day
  Shifted and changed like the dolphin's hues ;
The billows that rose and floated away,
  Were tinted and dyed like the rainbow's dews.
Oh ! life is gray when the heart is sad,
  And aflame when hope is enthroned above,
It has shifting colors when hours are glad,
  And is turned to gold by the light of love.
It is pale and haggard with doubts and fears,
  It is crimson with passion and black with sin ;
It ebbs and flows with the tide of years,
  And none can fathom the deeps within.

SEMI-CHORUS.

Like the phantom of a dream;
Like the spirit of a stream;
Breath of wind and foam of seas,
Passing o'er Symplegades;
Like a rainbow's broken light,
Sorrow-born of stainless white,
All its passions and desires
Violet and crimson fires;
Like the dawn that melts away,
Drowned in the heart of day;
Life is beautiful and brief;
Death the dropping of a leaf.

Weep ye that the flower is dead,
All its bloom and fragrance shed ?
Do ye murmer, do ye sigh,
That the sunset left the sky ?
And would ye renew the strife
Of the wonder we call life ?
What so beautiful and fair
As the blue and vacant air ?
What so measureless and deep
As a sweet and dreamless sleep ?
What though never more shall stir
Feeling in the breast of her,
Now so murmurless and still ?
She has drank and had her fill
Of the wine of mysteries,
Yet has tasted not the lees.
As the glitter of a spark
Lives a moment in the dark;
As the echo of a sound
Rises hollow from the ground,
And a transient moment fills
All the vale between the hills;
Life, the shadow of the wings
Brooding on insensate things;
Passes from the world of form
Back into the cosmic storm.
Like an arrow it has fled,
By an unseen archer sped;
And before the hand of Fate,
Earth is inarticulate;
Nor can man the gods resist,
Driven from the world like mist.
Still arise, serene and far,
Heaven's torches, star on star;
Still the moon her splendor throws
On the ocean whence she rose,
 And the sea-wind breaks and blows;
Still the mountain bulwarks stand

Round the city, dark and grand;
Simois and Scamander run
To the ocean, never done;
Still, in passing days, the year
Drops its withered blossoms here.
But the soul alone is dumb
When its flowering time is come;
And the heart that love has stirred,
Answers not an echoing word.
If the full-orbed moon should fail,
Or the twilight linger pale,
If the streams should cease to flow,
Or the winds forget to blow,
It were not so sad or strange
As the silence of this change.
What are all the garnered sheaves
Of the years but scattered leaves?
What are deeds of power and fame,
But a swift-extinguished flame?
What the joys of love and home,
But a spray of broken foam?
What the glory we have won,
But the setting of the sun?

ÆNEAS.

Too true, alas! too sad and true your words.
What deeds of might can stay the common doom
Of all the pride and glory of the world?
Behold the fallen fortunes of our Troy.
Even as Penthesilea when she came
White-browed and queenly to the fatal field,
Was our loved city fair and beautiful;
And in the unequal combat she will fall
As fell this maid; her altars will be stripped,
Her temples overthrown, her stately halls
Despoiled and ruined; and the household gods
Homeless amid their broken images.
Oh! mother, if thy voice is ever heard

Among the counsels of the wiser gods,
Lift it to save the city of thy son.
If we should wander forth from this our home,
What other land would have such fruitful fields,
Such sparkling rivers and such sunny skies?
Though all the beauty of the world were found
In some enchanted garden where the gods
Came down from heaven to breathe the fragrant air,
Where color, scent, and music all combined
Their several witcheries to charm the sense;
Yet were it not so sweet and dear as home.
Methinks if I were lifted to the heights
And set to banquet with the deathless gods,
Forbidden evermore to cast my eyes
Earthward upon the city that I love,
The nectar and ambrosia could not quench
The thirst and hunger of the human heart
For the familiar and remembered scenes.
Oh! land made sacred by dear memories
Of love and sorrow and of birth and death,
Even as the eyes and hands and lips and hair
Of mother to her infant, are thy hills,
Mountains, and plains, and rivers to thy sons.
Within thy bosom have we fallen asleep
And safely dreamed our hopes and griefs and joys;
And shall we wake to feel thy arms no more,
And stumble in the darkness and cry out,
Walking strange paths unguided and alone?
Loved Ilium, the walls our fathers built
Yet guard the heights of thine Acropolis,
The marble palace of thine aged king,
Homes of thy children, temples of thy gods.
Still from thy Pergamos and towers we see
The fertile plain of Troy, the triple stream
That rolls its tawny waters from the heights
Of Ida many-fountained to the sea.
And still the beeches and the olive-trees
Cluster about thee; and across the plain

The hills and mountains purple with the mist
Rise grand and beautiful; while in the west,
In crimson waves of sunset swims the peak
That lifts its head from far Ægean isles.
Against the portals of the Scaean Gate
Rises and falls the ceaseless tide of war.
How long will Ilium upon her hill
Stand like a rock amid the rushing waves?
How soon, alas! with rent and broken sails
Sink as a ship beneath the furious storm?
Was it for this that ancient Ilus came,
Following the rainbow cow, and where it lay
Built the fair city; and was it for this
The great Palladium fell before his tent,
Sent to him by the kindly hand of Zeus?
In the right hand it held a lifted lance,
Emblem of prowess in the city's sons;
A spindle and a distaff in the left,
Sign that her daughters would be chaste and true.
Upon the Pergamos fair temples rose
To Zeus, Athene, and the god of morn;
The many-chambered palace of the king,
And shrines and altars to the deathless gods;
About the palace clustered many homes,
And mighty walls and watch-towers girt about
The city, like the armour of a king.
In vain, in vain the glory of the Past;
In vain the struggles of the nine long years
The Achaean hosts have camped across the stream.
What god was wroth when fickle Paris saw
The lovely Helen and with swift-sailed ship
Bore her away from Menelaus' halls?
How many of the Trojan heroes fall,
How many women weep with unbound hair,
While children sob not knowing why they grieve.
Hector is dead; and unavenged the deed
That woke the gods to anger; now this maid
Lies white and silent underneath the stars.

Even the prowess of the Amazons,
Mighty among the nations of the world,
Could not avail to stay the course of fate.

CHORUS.

We have worshipped the moon with our hymns,
   And armed we have moved in the dance;
When the dusk of the twilight dims,
   And the world grows fair in her glance.
We have lifted her altars and shrines,
   We have builded her temples and fanes,
Where the glory of Ephesus shines,
   And the pride of our prowess remains.
The city we founded and built,
   With its walls and its ramparts and towers;
And the blood of the sacrifice spilt,
   And wreathed the fair altars with flowers.
We come of Olympian race,
   From Ares our splendor and might;
We are swift in the hunt and the chase,
   We are dauntless and strong in the fight.
With the axe and the lance and the bow,
   We move as a wind that is swift ;
We scatter the ranks of the foe,
   And leave them as sea-weed and drift.
Where flourish the fig-tree and beech,
   And the Hellespont breaks on the shore,
They have harkened the words of our speech;
   They have vanished our lances before.
And where the Ægean's blue waves
   Flow soft on his vine-laden isles,
We have made for our enemies graves,
   We have withered the bloom of their smiles.
In Hellas, Arabia, Thrace,
   Æthiopia, farthest of lands,
They have darkened at sight of our face,
   In vain they have lifted their hands.
Oh ! where are the strength and the might

That were given our armies of old ?
Oh ! where are the lances that smite,
　Now the heat of the battle is cold ?
Not so when Hippolyte died,
　Not so when Antiope fled;
Then Heracles humbled his pride,
　And Athens was filled with her dead.
But our leader, the bravest of queens,
　Our maiden, the fairest of maids,
From the noise and the pain of these scenes,
　Has gone unavenged to the shades.
Oh ! where are the arrows that flew,
　Oh ! where are the shields that were strong ?
Oh ! where is the battle-axe true,
Oh ! where are the lances that slew,
　And the arms to avenge us this wrong ?

ÆNEAS.

Who will avenge you now that Troy no more
Humbles her enemies, but bows her head
To the foul insults of the haughty Greeks ?

CHORUS.

How they have wronged us, harken thou the tale,
And how they fled before the Amazons.
One day, Hippolyte, the fair and strong,
Queen of the Amazons, on silken couch
In her apartments, whiled away the hours,
Looking with dreaming eyes upon the sea,
From whose blue billows breaking on the shore,
Came the cool breath of winds and with them blown,
The smell of salt and sea-weed; gently stirred
The queen's soft-flowing garments and her hair,
Falling in silken masses o'er her breast.
The sun-kissed sky blushed red and shot a gleam
That lit the whiteness of her cheek and brow.
To her came Heracles, his matchless form
And godlike features beautiful and strong

With strength and beauty as of mountain-oak,
Or the Nemean lion that he slew.
Eight labors had his mighty arm performed,
And on a ninth his crafty mind was bent.
Eurystheus commanded him to bring
The girdle of the queen, that Ares gave,
That made her mighty on the battle-field.
Matchless the hero's courage, yet he feared
To meet Hippolyte in open strife.
Long had he lingered till the time was ripe
To win by strategy the longed-for prize.
At sight of him she rose upon her arm,
And raised the hand that hung upon her couch,
That he might lift and lay it to his breast.
Then sank the hero low beside the queen,
And to her heart she laid the kingly head
And with her clinging hand caressed his hair.
"Hippolyte, I came to say farewell."
The voice was low and tender as the wind
That sings at twilight hour the dirge of day.
But to her ear more welcome were the shout
Of sea-winds and the fury of the storm.
"Tomorrow, at the break of day, my sails
Filled with the wind, must leave these happy shores
And seek again the land that I forsook
To be with thee, too dear, too beautiful."
The sun dropped into darkness and the gleam
Faded from out her face and left it pale
As the moon looking for Endymion.

"Oh ! leave me not; what is the world but thee,
And what is life but heart-throbs beating fast
In rhythm to thy words ? forsake me not,
Lest all the golden splendor of the day
And molten beauty of the sun-touched sea
Turn black before mine eyes; lest all the trees,
Whose soft leaves whisper love and happiness,
Stir only with the strain of funeral hymns;

Lest all the radiant fairness of the dawn
Darken and tremble back behind the hills.
Oh ! leave me not to memory and tears.
What worth were life without thee, how could I,
Desolate, widowed of my summer joy,
Fill the slow measure of the days and nights
Without thy presence? how could I awake
And rise to face the morning with my pain?"

"Think only of the joy that we have known,
Nor let it grieve thee that the hour is past.
Where is the glory that was wont to move
Thy spirit?   Where the noise of battle-field,
The clash of lances and the clang of shields
Stricken from alien hands upon the ground?
Soon in the eager combat wilt thou feel
Swift as of old, and warm, the pulse of life;
But, fair Hippolyte, do not forget,
In battle scenes, these softer moments spent
Beside the Thermodon with Heracles."

"Forget ! ye gods, the whole of life will be
One aching memory, one passionate prayer
To heaven for thy love and thy return.
Nor ever will the battle intervene
To hide the memory of thy lips and brow.
If I could keep thy heart from growing cold,
Or give assurance of my faithfulness,
No wish so great but I would gladly grant.
My heart, my life, my soul I gave to thee,
And fain my hapless love would give thee more."

The girdle slipped and loosened fell her robes
Swelling with the pent passion of her heart.

"If I might keep this girdle as a sign,"—
She started and grew paler than the snow—
"That thou art constant; and a gift to bring
The memory of thy love like cooling springs
In the deep-hid recesses of my heart;

This girdle that seems even a part of thee,
That held thy form as erst these clasping arms;
Then would it be a talisman to keep
My love still fragrant as fresh lotus-blooms."

She turned her face a moment from his sight.
" Is this alone the gift to satisfy
Thy love and longing ? Arrows swift and bows,
Lances and helmets, axes, crescent shields,
All weapons for the battle-field are here
For thee to choose from; take them all and go,
A god to war; and think, when aliens fall,
Hippolyte is with thee in the fight."

   And is the girdle more than life to thee,
Than heart and soul ? then must the god that gave
Be dearer to thy love than Heracles."

Swifter than flight of winds she rose and laid
Her hands on either shoulder, looking straight
(So queenly was she), in the hero's eyes;
" Tomorrow when the sun first stirs the hills
From their dark dreams, and brightens all the sea,
While yet the streets are empty of the throng,
Will I go down to see thee spread thy sails,
And bring the girdle and give it to thy hands.
Another day mine eyes must look on thee;
Not lose thee now." She turned from him and wept;
A moment felt the pressure of his arms,
His breath like stirring wings that fanned her cheek,
A moment heard the murmur of his voice,
Like gentle waters broken on the sand;
Then sank upon her silken couch, alone.

But Heracles sped seaward through the streets,
Seeking his white-sailed ships; and roused the youths
That came with him from Greece and bade them make
All ready for the journey in the morn.
Meantime did Hera, looking down on earth,
See Heracles victorious in the ninth

Of his great labors; and her anger grew.
Then like an Amazon the goddess came,
And through the silent streets from house to house,
Went noiselessly and woke the warrior maids.
"Tomorrow morning," said the artful queen
Of heaven, "go with your lances to the shore
Where rock the foreign ships upon the tide;
And you will find them ready to set sail,
As sea-birds poising and spreading out their wings;
And on the beach, your queen Hippolyte
And Heracles, who thinks to bear her hence,
As sign of victory o'er the Amazons."

Purple the morning rose upon the hills
And o'er the sea; the queen Hippolyte,
With girdled robes and gleaming tresses bound,
Sped swiftly through the lone and empty streets,
Scarce echoing where her sandalled feet fell soft,
And came where rocked the ships upon the tide,
And Heracles stood waiting on the beach,
Fair as a god; while yet they lingered, loath
To say the heavy word of parting, came
Like flocks of white-winged birds, the Amazons,
With shields and lances, shouting battle-cries.
Then turned the wrathful hero to the queen,
Who shrank aghast before his lifted arm
And the good lance that glittered in the sun.
"What treachery of thine has armed the land
Against me? Is the girdle worth my life,
That thou shouldst fill the streets with Amazons,
And bar my passage to the waiting ships?"

She raised her arm as to with-hold the blow.
"Dost fear to die who would have slain thy love,
And ask for mercy him thou wouldst not spare?"

From her white quivering throat there broke a sob,
A sound as made by a death-wounded dove.
"I ask no quarter; for an Amazon

Scorns it; but only that thou knowest me true;
Why the armed women follow to the ships,
I know not; I have lain upon my couch,
Alone with sorrow and my thoughts of thee.
Slay me unarmed; but do not deem me false.
Strike to the heart that loves thee." Here she drew
Her robe aside and waited for the blow.

It fell; and as the blood leaped to his lance,
"Farewell, false queen," he said; and when she sank,
Tore from her robe the girdle and turned away,
Nor saw the arms and eyes that followed him,
Nor heard the dying whisper that forgave.

Like the wild roarings of a hundred winds,
Or mingled thunder of unnumbered storms,
The clamor of the Amazons arose
At sight of slain Hippolyte; they swept
The trembling Greeks before them to the ships;
But many lay upon the beach, no more
To look on Hellas; even Heracles
Fled with his shivered shield and broken lance;
But still the girdle hung upon his arm;
And as the sails spread out before the breeze,
Backward he looked upon the Amazons,
And the heaped corses of his slaughtered friends,
That strewed the shore; pursuing arrows flew
And stirred the troubled and broken waves to foam,
And rent the sails and quivered in the deck.

ÆNEAS.

Much have you suffered from the haughty Greeks,
And yet your glory has been great indeed;
Since hardly the Hellenic heroes fled
Back with their lives; and even Heracles,
In fraud, not battle, overcame your queen.

CHORUS.

Greater the glory after Theseus

Carried the brave Antiope away.
Scarcely had Heracles returned to Greece,
Ere came the Athenian hero with his troops,
And sought to plunder and destroy the land.
The warriors were unarmed; but at the cry
Of battle, swift prepared them for the fight,
Led by the fair Antiope, whose form,
Slender and stately as a mountain fir,
Moved ever at the front; mid dust of war,
And flash of steel, and hillocks of the slain
Who fell beneath her strokes, the hero saw
And loved her; far behind her were her troops;
About her she had placed a wall of dead,
And stood within the army of her foes.
At Theseus' word they formed a circle round
The queen, and he advanced with lifted lance;
But swift her battle-axe cleft through his mail,
The while she lifted up the crescent shield
And turned aside his stroke; then had she slain
The adventurous hero, but his friends drew near,
And though they fell before her like the rain,
Yet came they on until her strength was spent,
And Theseus, gathering her within his arms,
Bore her unconscious from the battle-field.
Then had the Amazons destroyed the host
Of Grecian heroes, but they fled and reached
The ships and spread their sails before the breeze.

Swifter than flight of homeward-faring bird
They fled; meanwhile, the Amazons prepared
For a long war and followed them to Greece.
Hellas lay blooming like a garden planned
For pleasure of the gods; the vineyards blushed
For Dionysius' coming; and the fig,
Olive, and lemon gave such luscious fruit,
Scarce the ambrosia of the gods excelled.
For many days the women warriors roved
The land and plundered all the blossoming fields;

Making their homes like nymphs and dryades
In the deep woodlands and beside the streams.
At last they came to Athens; through her gates
Poured, a resistless flood; the city rose
As out of sleep and put her armor on.
The streets were filled with fighting; at the base
Of the Acropolis raged fierce the war;
And surely would the mighty Amazons
Have left but smoking ruins where now stands
The templed city; but Athene saw,
And with her arms and awful aegis came
And led the fight; and only from her wrath
Did the invaders flee without the gates.

ÆNEAS.

Well were it had the city been destroyed
And lovely Hellas wrested from their hands.
Always their arms are lifted up to smite;
Always their feet are following alien paths
Seeking new conquest; I am weary grown
Of war and battle; sweet the household shrines,
The peaceful hours, and smiles of those we love.
Oh! dear and sweet is home as summer dreams
That haunt the meadows and enchanted woods,
When swings the bird upon the swaying bough,
Full-throated, tremulous with breaking song;
When sleep the winds upon the sunny slopes,
And in the grasses where the blossoms break
In white and purple splendor; dear and sweet
The soft familiar voices that we know
As the faint music that the sea-nymphs hear,
When the winds, lightly passing, kiss the waves,
Nor stir their bosoms with ungentle breath.
And sweet and dear the faces that have grown
Into our love, as flowers that breathe a balm
Upon the quiet air; as stars that shine
To startle into loveliness the night.
But we must die or see the homes we love

Ashes and ruins; while the faces fade,
As flowers that furl their petals in the sun,
Or stars that shrink affrighted from the day;
While die the mellow voices like the sound
Of plaintive echoes in a dim recess
Banked in with thymy slopes and misty hills;
Or as the fading foot-falls of the gods,
Who seek at dewy night their earthly loves,
Melt into silence at the stir of dawn.
Much have the Grecians wronged you, but your
    homes
Still stand unplundered by the Thermodon.

CHORUS.

Our homes, alas! with her who blest them gone;
The fairest, bravest of our mighty queens,
Sweetest of those by foreign heroes slain,
Wisest and best and strongest in the fight.
Where find we now a queen to lead our hosts
To conquest?   Where a maiden that will rule
So nobly in our city by the sea?
Our homes are filled with mourning and our land
Louder with lamentations than with winds
And billows breaking on the glimmering shore.

MESSENGER.

Let the moon veil her silver face in clouds,
And on the swift feet of the summer winds,
Speed back to heaven and leave earth desolate.
Let Artemis take down the crescent shield
From the calm skies and break it into stars;
For haply they will light the path of man,
Nor lend their torches to his funeral pyre.
The shield is broken on the battle-plain;
The queen of earth is vanished into night.
And let the silver tongues of all the winds
That murmur in Æolus' caverns, break
Into lamenting; let the brazen clash

Of heavy billows roll tempestuous
Lashed to a storm of passion and despair.
Let all the cedars on the mountain-tops,
Stooping to hear the faint voice of the winds,
Whisper and sigh the story to the night.
Perchance the oreads will hear the tale,
And murmur it to lovers when they sit
Upon the mountain-side beneath the stars;
Or happy goddessess and women warm
In clasping arms, shudder at thought of her,
Cold with the kisses of the river-god;
The foam upon her lips and in her hair;
The chill within her bosom, while the night,
Upon her eyes drops starless 'neath the waves.

CHORUS.

What mean you by the river and the foam?

MESSENGER.

Ye gods, if all the fountains and the streams
Were human tears, yet were they not enough
To greet the tale that trembles to be told,
Crouching behind the portal of my lips,
Monstrous, to spring and prey upon your hearts.
Already like a polished pearl she lay,
Perfumed and shrouded for the sacred rites,
And lovely as the memory of a dream;
While far-off Charon steered his phantom barque
The hither side of Styx; and backward rolled
The gates of Hades, waiting for her soul.
Peace is the meed of him who leaves the world,
Having lived to the end of some good thing,
Accomplished it at last, or died for it;
And having given his body to the gods
With sacrificial rites and pious prayers.
So on her features lay a holy calm,
As shine the moon-beams on a quiet lake,
Deep in the heart of night; so still the brow,

So still and white and motionless the form,
When life and love and battle all are done.
But never will her spirit walk serene
Among the shadows of the under-world,
Till the slow circle of a hundred years
Her homeless feet have trodden on the shore.
The waters of Scamander bear the maid
Paler than foam of billows to the sea.

CHORUS.

Alas! that we should live and hear the tale.
But who so daring he would tempt the gods,
By such a deed; thrice hated, thrice accursed?

MESSENGER.

'Twas Diomed, the pitiless, the bold,
Who wounded Aphrodite on the hand,
And even sent the mighty god of war
With groans to heaven; Diomed, who stole
With wise Ulysses to the Trojan camp,
As all lay sleeping, Rhesus slew, and led
His famous steeds in triumph to the Greeks.
In the dark stillness of the night he came,
As vulture swooping on the slaughtered dove,
And like a timid flock the watchers fled.
Fierce with the hatred of the haughty race,
And mad for vengeance, in his arms he raised
The lovely sleeper from her perfumed couch,
And in the darkness speeding like the wind,
Bore her to old Scamander's reedy banks;
And there, while Artemis with unmoved face
Looked from her silver throne amid the stars,
He lifted high the maiden in his arms,
And cast her from him in the sobbing waves,
That broke the phantom image of the moon,
And sighed and murmured to the heavy night.
Then would one say that Artemis indeed
Had left her throne to slumber on the stream,

While still her silver shield hung in the sky;
For lovely as the goddess that she loved,
The queen lay rocking on the yellow breast
Of old Scamander; while the low-voiced winds
Chanted the strophes of her bridal hymn.

CHORUS.

But where were they, the Trojans, while he fled
With Penthesilea through the night and gloom?

MESSENGER.

Fleetly they followed, but his feet were winged,
And as they neared the margin of the stream,
They saw her unbound hair, like floating reeds,
Upon the water, and her face upraised
As if in pleading, to the archer-queen.
A moment only; then the waves flowed on,
Serene, unbroken, pallid with the moon;
And nodding by the river in the breeze,
The lotus and the snow-white asphodel
Amid the rushes gleamed like fallen stars.
But meanwhile Diomed had sped away,
And all in vain they searched the river-bank,
And open plain; the robber left no trace
More than the wind upon undrifted snow.
Slumber the gods that things like this can be?
How often have men cried to them in vain,
Lifted imploring eyes and heavy hearts,
Rich sacrifices spread and spilled the wine,
Wreathed woodland fanes and altars with fair
  flowers
And heard no answer to their murmured prayers
But mocking laughter of the wanton winds,
Playing with blown wet tresses of the nymphs;
Or happy pipe of birds in leafy nests,
Or sobbing shudder of the breaking sea.
Calm as the stars and colder than the moon,
More swiftly changing than the star of day,

Showing their faces now in kindly deeds
And hiding them anon to leave us lost
In night and tempest; changeless are the gods
In youth immortal and eternal bloom;
But changeful unto man as yonder bow
That hangs its silver crescent up tonight,
And erelong broadens to a Grecian shield,
Then breaks and fades and vanishes away.
And yet men pray and worship, seeking still
A strength to stay their weakness and a light
To kindle the quenched torches that they bear.
'Tis not the gods that slumber, but mankind;
'Tis not the eternal changes, but the soul.
We are but children sobbing in the night,
And feeling in the darkness for the breast
Of universal Life; Oh ! blest is he,
Who hears the mighty beatings of her heart,
And lays his throbbing temples on the calm
White bosom, while his lips, in eager draught,
Are filled with wisdom from her sacred fount.
He hears the songs unhymned of mortal bard,
Wild strains of music swept from vibrant lyres
Whose strings are thought and passion; and he sees
Above the rosy scarf of Iris' robes,
The glimmer of a ray unknown to earth.
So Man, were he but childlike in his love,
Faithful to all the promptings of the gods,
Would see them face to face, nor seek in vain
To follow them and clasp their knees in prayer.
Alas! his eyes, turned often from the light,
Are dazzled by its splendor and are blind.
His soul went dreaming on a summer day
And found the isle of Circe in the sea,
And drank the wine of sin; and so his gaze
Fell from the glory of the stars to earth.

ÆNEAS.

The night grows deeper and the stars come out,

A million torches for the funeral rites
Of the slain queen; the sea-winds sing sad strains,
And all the waves are sobbing on the shore
With lamentation for the lovely dead.
Earth, night, and ocean bid her spirit rest.
But on the Greeks the gods avenge this wrong.
Bow down their haughty heads and bend their knees,
Darken the splendor of their glancing spears,
And stain their limbs and armor with the dust.
Make widows of their wives that watch and wait
In vain to see their white sails from afar,
O'er the horizon loom like floating clouds,
Or spreading wings of sea-birds; make their sons,
Sobbing and clinging to their mothers' robes,
Orphans that vainly babble of their sires,
Not knowing they will never see them more.
Crumble their walls and strike their bulwarks down,
Lay low their citadels and blight their fields,
Scatter their armies as the chaff that flies
Before strong winds; make desolate their homes,
Ruin their temples and their wayside shrines,
Make all their land from sea to sounding sea,
Cities and valleys and the fertile plains,
Woodlands and forests and mountain-heights,
A waste and ruin; make their people flee
And find no refuge; bind the chains of slaves
Upon their wives and children, while they fall
Before a pitiless enemy and their limbs
Unburied, feed the vulture and the kite;
And make their name, once splendid with renown,
Forgotten from the annals of the world.

FIRST SEMI-CHORUS.

Where is the maiden peerless,
Mighty in war and fearless,
Lovely and fair as the dawn ?

SECOND SEMI-CHORUS.

Under the rippling water,

White from Achaean slaughter,
Slumbers the Amazons' daughter,
  Torn and haggard and wan.

FIRST SEMI-CHORUS.

Is it the stars that shiver
Their silver lights in the river,
  Is it the moon's pale gleam?

SECOND SEMI-CHORUS.

Those are her eyes that brighten,
Those are her arms that whiten,
Those are her features that lighten
  The gloom of the shadowy stream.

FIRST SEMI-CHORUS.

Is that the drifting rushes,
Is that a flower that brushes
  Its petals upon the waves?

SECOND SEMI-CHORUS.

Those her unfilleted tresses,
Lips that were made for caresses,
Fingers the water-god presses,
  Beauty the water-god laves.

CHORUS.

Rippled and stirred by the wind's faint flurries,
Onward the undulent current hurries.
The fret of life and its ceaseless worries
  Sleep in the breast of the silent queen;
Turned is the soul from its high endeavor,
The old world-voices are hushed forever,
  Her feet have trodden the paths unseen.

FIRST SEMI-CHORUS.

Under the faint star-candles,
Night in her silver sandals,

Speeds to the glowing Morn;
Morn as a bride receives her,
Robes of the sunrise weaves her,
Slays and kisses and leaves her,
  Dim and pallid and worn.

SECOND SEMI-CHORUS.

So did the maiden hasten,
Swift to avenge and chasten,
  Strong to the battle-plain;
The heart of Achilles knew her;
The hand of Achilles slew her;
With robes of the dust to strew her,
  He left her among the slain.

FIRST SEMI-CHORUS.

As tiger from mountain fastness,
As monster from ocean vastness,
  Came the fierce Diomed.

SECOND SEMI-CHORUS.

Far from the arms of lover,
With only the waves for cover,
With wails of the wind above her,
  Slumbers the lovely dead.

CHORUS.

Life's sweet guerdon her spirit misses.
Never for her our earthly blisses,
Never the touch of love's warm kisses,
  Only the chill of the river's lips;
Never for her the bridal tapers,
Only the mist and gloomy vapors,
  Only the night and love's eclipse.

FIRST SEMI-CHORUS.

Far from the flowing Scamander,
Alone does her shadow wander,
  On shores of the murmurless stream;

And still does she shudder and shiver
At sight of the desolate river,
Her spirit athrob and aquiver,
　As under the spell of a dream.

SECOND SEMI-CHORUS.

Lo ! Charon looks gloomy before him,
Unmoved that her white hands implore him,
　Unheeding her prayers and her tears;
No matter how lonely her flight is,
No matter how heavy the night is,
While over the river Thersites
　The shadowy boatman steers.

FIRST SEMI-CHORUS.

Oh ! never the queen will greet us,
Laid low by the son of Thetis,
　Dishonored by Diomed;

SECOND SEMI-CHORUS.

And never the fire that dashes
On pyre, and on altar flashes,
Will give us the sacred ashes
　For memory of the dead.

CHORUS.

Her deeds are done and her words are spoken,
The wine is quaffed and the bowl is broken;
Oh ! what is Life that it leaves no token,
　Oh ! what is Death that it makes no sign?
Are they the real that blossoms and passes,
The flowers that fade and the withered grasses,
　Or only the shadows of form divine?

FIRST SEMI-CHORUS.

Lo! a white face uplifted,
Lo! a fair body drifted
　Out on the rushing stream;

SECOND SEMI-CHORUS.

Mad are the waves with motion,
Drunk with the wild wind's potion,
Lost in infinite ocean,
    Faded as fades a dream.

FIRST SEMI-CHORUS.

Softly the nymphs are risen,
Purple their tresses glisten,
    Wide are their purple eyes;
Parting the waves asunder,
Mutely they look and wonder;
Never such beauty under
    Billowy seas and skies.

SECOND SEMI-CHORUS.

Even the gloomy Poseidon
Watches her glimmer and glide on,
    Whiter than spray and foam;
Thinks her a goddess in slumber,
Of the immortal number,
Careless of sea-weeds' cumber,
    Strayed from Olympian home.

CHORUS.

Hark! the winds and the waves are slowly
Chanting their hymns for the dead, who lowly
Lays her head on the couch unholy,
    Spread with the drift and slime of the deep;
Down in the gloom the oceanids pour all
Their hidden wealth of pearls and of coral
. To deck the queen in her silent sleep.

FIRST SEMI-CHORUS.

Peace to the maiden lonely,
Peace to her soul, for only
    Prayers we can give, and tears;
Lost to the light and splendor,

Silence and gloom attend her;
May the Eumenides send her
    Peace in the pulseless years.

SECOND SEMI-CHORUS.

Never a smile will cheer her,
Never a lover near her,
    Never a face from the throng;
Never a note of laughter
Ripple and sparkle after;
Never the wind will waft her
    Words and the splendor of song.

FIRST SEMI-CHORUS.

Gone is breath from the bosom,
Gone as dew from the blossom,
    Gone as dawn from the hills;

SECOND SEMI-CHORUS.

Slowly the dim hours wear on;
Only from swamp and barren,
Lo ! the voice of the heron
    Night and the silence fills.

CHORUS.

Oh! that we left our fields to the reaper,
Oh! that we prayed to Zeus, the Keeper,
Oh! that we mourn the beautiful sleeper,
    Silent and cold in the cold still sea;
Would we had left not our woodland chases,
Would we had sought not the foreign faces,
    Would we had come not, lost Troy, to thee.

FIRST SEMI-CHORUS.

There does the night bring easeful
Hours and dream visions peaceful,
    Breathing of dew and shade;
There in the green fields hilly,

White in the moon-light stilly,
Slumber the rose and lily,
  Stainless and unafraid.

SECOND SEMI-CHORUS.

Not the tumult of battle,
Not the clamor and rattle,
  Not the flashing of spears;
Only the cool dim noises,
Night's intangible voices;
Haply the wind rejoices,
  And but a wood-nymph hears.

CHORUS.

Oh ! for the sea and mountain,
Oh ! for the stream and fountain,
  Oh ! for the fields of home;
Moon o'er the lake arisen,
Waters that break and glisten,
Valleys that wake and listen,
  Woodlands, we come, we come.